Smokey's Big Day

By
DeHaven Jacque Alexander

Illustrated by
LADEHU

Copyright © 2024 by DeHaven Jacque Alexander

ISBN: 978-1-965498-17-0

All rights reserved. No part of this book may be reproduced or transmitted in any form or by any means, electronic or mechanical, including photocopying, recording, or by any information storage and retrieval system, without permission in writing from the copyright owner.

The views expressed in this work are solely those of the author and do not necessarily reflect the views of the publisher, and the publisher disclaims any responsibility for them.

To order additional copies of this book, contact:
Proisle Publishing Services LLC
39-67 58th 1st Floor Woodside
New York, NY 11377, USA
Phone: (+1 646-480-0129)
info@proislepublishing.com

To my three sons,
DeHaven Jr., DeShaun and DeAngelo
and to my wife,
Claudia Alexander

Smokey is a small baby cat who loves his mommy and daddy and loves to chew on shoes. Smokey has two stuffed animals he loves to play with. Ruff and Pee Wee are the same size as Smokey so he has a hard time trying to pull them off the bed.

Smokey's mother has a friend whose name is Tina. Tina has a dog named Puff. Now, Puff was a big fluffy dog who was very playful. When Smokey saw Puff, Smokey ran under the couch. He was very scared, so Smokey's mother told Tina to take Puff outside.

Smokey's mother had to reach under the couch and pull Smokey out because he was very scared. Smokey was scared to go outside but he loves to get in the window. He also loves to sit on the table.

One day Smokey's mother told Smokey's father, "We have to take Smokey to the doctor to get his shots." Now this was going to be a challenge because Smokey never goes outside. Smokey is scared to go outside. Smokey's father told Smokey's mother, "We Will put Smokey in a bag and take Smokey out of the house in the bag."

The day came when Smokey had to go to the doctor. It was snowing outside and it was cold. They decided since the weather was nasty it was probably best to take Smokey to the doctor on the train.

The morning came to take Smokey to the doctor. Smokey's father picked Smokey up and out him in a black bag. Smokey stuck his little head out of the bag. He was looking around at all the sights as they all walked down the street.

Smokey was also making the bag hard for his mother to carry so his father had to carry him as they got on the train. Smokey was just looking at his father wondering what was going on.

The three of them went uptown to the doctor's office. Now Smokey started to poke his head out of the bag as they walked up the street. Then they went to the wrong doctor's office.

Smokey started jumping around the bag so he could see what was going on. Smokey's mother told him that she had to put him back in the bag so they could find the right doctor's office.

They continue to walk up the street and Smokey again tried to jump out of the bag. Smokey's father had to put him back down in the bag. Smokey's father carried Smokey in his arms while Smokey stayed in the bag.

When they walked into the doctor's office, Smokey's mother went to the front desk and checked Smokey in. The nurse told Smokey's parents to bring him to the back so the doctor could look at him since Smokey was a baby. The doctor told them that they were going to keep Smokey overnight.

Smokey started to cry. His mother and father were sad too so they gave Smokey a kiss and told him not to cry, that they would be back to get him the very next day.

They left Smokey and went home since they were going to pick Smokey up the next morning. When the next day came, Smokey's mother went to get Smokey.

His father had to go to work. Smokey's mother went up to the doctor's office to get Smokey. He looked at her and Smokey was happy to see his mother. She picked him up and carried him in her arms out of the doctor's office. They walked down the street and got on the train and Smokey stuck his little head out of the bag on the way home.

When they got home, Smokey's mother took him out of the bag and he jumped on the bed and went to sleep. He was tired. Later, his father came home from work and played with Smokey and they all ate dinner and fell asleep.

Today, Smokey is very happy. He is sitting in the window watching the little kids playing outside.

Smokey is a little kitten who knows exactly what he likes and doesn't like. Smokey likes to play. He likes to sit and stare out windows. But Smokey doesn't like to go outside. He is too scared. No one can make him go outside. But now it's time for Smokey to get his shots. He needs to go out and see the veterinarian. Will he have the courage to go? Will his parents be able to get him there? What adventures will he encounter along the way?

Smokey's Big Day, by DeHaven Jacque Alexander, is an entertaining and warmly illustrated story for preschoolers.

About The Author

DEHAVEN JACQUE ALEXANDER is a passionate storyteller and cat lover, as seen in his children's book, Smokey's Big Day. A graduate of Cameron University with a degree in Criminal Justice, Dehaven also served in the military at Fort Sill, where he was a boxing team member. Now living in Las Vegas, he is a fashion designer who continues to explore his creativity through fashion classes at UNLV. Dehaven's unique blend of experiences-from military service to fashion design-adds a special touch to his enchanting stories.

PROISLE PUBLISHING
SERVICES LLC

BARCODE

www.ingramcontent.com/pod-product-compliance
Lightning Source LLC
LaVergne TN
LVHW050139080526
838202LV00061B/6533